William J. Thoms

Hannah Lightfoot. Queen Charlotte & the Chevalier d'Eon.

Dr. Wilmot's Polish princess.

William J. Thoms

Hannah Lightfoot. Queen Charlotte & the Chevalier d'Eon.
Dr. Wilmot's Polish princess.

ISBN/EAN: 9783337168261

Printed in Europe, USA, Canada, Australia, Japan

Cover: Foto ©Andreas Hilbeck / pixelio.de

More available books at **www.hansebooks.com**

HANNAH LIGHTFOOT.

QUEEN CHARLOTTE & THE CHEVALIER D'EON.

DR. WILMOT'S POLISH PRINCESS.

BY

WILLIAM J. THOMS, F.S.A.

REPRINTED WITH SOME ADDITIONS, FROM 'NOTES AND QUERIES'

LONDON:

W. G. SMITH, 32 WELLINGTON STREET, STRAND, W.C.

1867.

PREFACE.

THESE Notes on the story of Hannah Lightfoot have been reprinted in compliance with suggestions from several quarters, that the proofs which they contain of the utter groundlessness of the scandal should be preserved in a more convenient form than the pages of *Notes and Queries*, in which they originally appeared.

A writer, who has obviously paid much attention to the subject, while admitting that the evidence of the want of truth in the story, which is here adduced, is conclusive, thinks there are two statements respecting it which require further canvassing. One is Mr. Steinman Steinman's (*N. & Q.* 2nd S. i. 222) statement that a portrait of Miss Axford, the Fair Quaker, painted by Sir Joshua Reynolds, exists at Knole, and the other, the statement of E. D. (*N. & Q.* 1st S. x. 430) that Dr. James Dalton, of the Madras Medical Service, married a daughter of Hannah Lightfoot by George III.

How the portraits at Knole, said to represent 'Miss Axford, the Fair Quaker,' came to be so designated I know not, but I would remark that that mythic personage, the 'Fair Quaker,' has never been described as a *Miss* Axford. I may add, on the authority of my friend Mr. Scharf, that the picture does not represent a Quakeress, for the lady is dressed in white satin with pink bows; like the portraits of *La Baccelli*, and the *Schinderlin*, also at Knole, and painted by Sir Joshua, it is believed to have been added to the collection by the third Duke of Dorset; and like those portraits, is probably that of one of his mistresses.

With reference to the Dalton descendants from the supposed connection, I would remind the reader, that another family residing at the Cape of Good Hope claim the same origin (2 S. *N. & Q.* 89); and I may add that, while these papers were in course of publication in *Notes and Queries*, no less than three other families, whose names I do not think it right to publish, have been mentioned to me as the undoubted descendants of the King and the Fair Quaker. But as the five families which claim such descent have no connection with each other, the reader will probably concur with me in the conviction that they have just as little connection with George III. and his supposed Quaker mistress. Whether the King has or has not been made the scapegoat for his father, as has been suggested, or any of his brothers, is not the question which I undertook to investigate.

40 St. George's Square, S.W.
May 1867.

CONTENTS.

———◦◇◦———

HANNAH LIGHTFOOT.

WHEN looking into that barefaced and impudent
fiction, the pretended marriage of Dr. Wilmot to the
Princess Poniatowski, to which I called the attention
of the readers of *Notes and Queries* in July 1866
(3rd S. x. p. 1), I found the name of Hannah Lightfoot so mixed up with the affair that I could scarcely
resist the conviction that the Fair Quaker* was as
mythical a personage as the Polish Princess.

The publication of Mr. Jesse's amusing *Memoirs
of the Life and Reign of George III.* has brought
before the public once more the alleged connection
and marriage between George III. and Hannah
Lightfoot.

Mr. Jesse, however, gives to some of the authorities
which he uses an amount of weight and credit which
a little consideration will show they by no means deserve. I propose, therefore, to point out upon what
a mass of contradictory statements the scandal is
founded, in the firm conviction that if my readers do
not go the length of rejecting the story altogether,
they will pause before they even believe that George

* 'Fair Quaker,' not Quakeress, was the name by which the young
lady was generally designated.

III. intrigued with Hannah Lightfoot; and will feel thoroughly convinced that there is not a shadow of truth in this alleged marriage, in which Mr. Jesse seems disposed to believe.

The first thing that strikes one as remarkable with regard to this piece of scandal is that no allusion to it is to be found (at least as far as I am able to trace) in any historical, political, or satirical work published during the lifetime of George III. Walpole, whose industry in collecting gossip equalled the delight with which he disseminated it, has no allusion to a story which he never could have known and kept secret; but, on the contrary, speaks of Prince George at the very time when this *liaison* must have existed, if it ever did exist, as ' bigoted, young, and *chaste*.' But from the year after that in which George III. died, the story has been continually reappearing in one or other of the many varied forms which it has assumed.

The subject is probably of sufficient interest to justify my reprinting such notices on the subject as have not already appeared in the columns of *Notes and Queries*. In the first, from *The Monthly Magazine* for April 1821, it will be observed the lady is spoken of as a Miss Wheeler.

All the world is acquainted with the attachment of *the late King* to a beautiful Quakeress *of the name of* WHEELER. The lady *disappeared on the royal marriage* in a way that has always been interesting because unexplained and mysterious. I have been told she is still alive, or was lately. As connected with the life of the late sovereign, the subject is curious; and any information through your pages would doubtless be agreeable to many of your readers. B.

Monthly Mag. April 1, 1821, vol. li. p. 523.

In the reply which this inquiry brought forth in

the July number of the magazine, the lady becomes a Miss Lightfoot; and the story is set forth with some incidents which I here content myself with printing in italics:—

Reminiscentia of remarkable Characters of the last Age:

HANNAH LIGHTFOOT

(The Fair Quaker).

[In consequence of the enquiry relative to this celebrated lady, in a late number, we have been favoured with the following letter from a respectable gentleman at Warminster, and we are promised further information. On enquiring of the Axford family, who still are respectable grocers on Ludgate Hill, we traced a son of the person alluded to in the letter, by his second wife, Miss Bartlett, and ascertained that the information of our correspondent is substantially correct. From him we learn that the lady *lived six weeks with her husband*, who was fondly attached to her, but one evening when he happened to be *from home, a coach and four* came to the door, when she was conveyed into it and carried off at a gallop, no one knew whither. It appears the husband was inconsolable at first, and at different times applied for information about his wife at Weymouth and other places, but died after sixty years in total ignorance of her fate. It has, however, been reported that *she had three sons* by her lover, since high in the army; that she was *buried at Islington under another name*, and even that she *is still alive*.]

Your correspondent enquires (in your magazine for April) for some account of the Fair Quaker who once engaged the affections of Prince George. Her name was not WHEELER, but HANNAH LIGHTFOOT. She lived with her father and mother at the corner of St. James' Market, who kept a shop there (I believe a linendraper's). The Prince had often noticed her in his way from Leicester House to St. James', and was struck with her person. Miss Chudleigh, late Duchess of Kingston, became his agent.

The royal lover's relations took alarm, and sent to enquire out a young man to marry her. Isaac Axford was shopman to Barton the grocer *on Ludgate Hill*, and used to chat with her when *she came to the shop to buy groceries*.

Perryn of Knightsbridge, it was said, furnished a place of meeting for the royal lover. An agent of Miss Chudleigh called on Axford, and proposed that on his marrying Hannah he should have a considerable sum of money.

Hannah staid a short time with her husband, when she was taken off in a carriage, and Isaac never saw her more. Axford learned that she was gone with Miss Chudleigh. Isaac was a poor-hearted fellow, or, by making a bustle about it, he might perhaps have secured to himself a good provision. He told me, when I last saw him, that he *presented a petition at St. James'*, which was not attended to; also that he had *received some money* from Perryn's assignees *on account of his wife*.

Isaac lived many years as a respectable grocer at Warminster, his native place, but retired from business before his death, which took place about five years ago, in the eighty-sixth year of his age.

Many years after Hannah was taken away, her husband, believing her dead, was married again to a Miss Bartlett of Keevel (N. Wilts), and by her succeeded to an estate at Chevrett of about 150*l.* a year. On the report reviving, a few years since, of his first wife's being still living, a Mr. Bartlett (first cousin to Isaac's second wife) claimed the estate on the plea of the invalidity of this second marriage.

It was said that the late Marquis of Bath, a little before his death, reported that she was then living, and the same has been asserted by other gentlemen of this neighbourhood.

Hannah was fair and pure, as far as ever I heard; but report says 'not the purest of all pures' in respect to the house of Mr. Perryn, who left her an annuity of 40*l.* a year. She was indeed considered as one of the beautiful women of her time, and rather disposed to *embonpoint*.

WARMINSTERIENSIS.

Warminster, 30 April 1821.

This statement did not appear satisfactory at least to one reader of the magazine, and accordingly WAR-MINSTERIENSIS was invited to explain the following contradictions in his statement; but no such explanation appears to have been offered:—

You and your readers, I feel no doubt, are particularly obliged by the communication of your intelligent correspondent *Warminsteriensis*, but as he has not been sufficiently explicit upon some points, I hope for my curiosity he will answer the following questions:—

1. Can your correspondent assign any reason for the Fair Quaker being sometimes called *Wheeler* and sometimes *Lightfoot*?

2. What was the motive that induced Miss Chudleigh to offer 'a considerable sum of money' to Isaac Axford to marry Hannah Lightfoot?

3. When and where did the marriage take place of Hannah Lightfoot, a Quaker, to I. Axford, and where is the evidence that she was the same Quaker who lived at the corner of St. James' Market, and was admired by Prince George?

4. Where was she carried off from in the coach and four?

5. Where and at what time was the law-suit?

6. Did Mr. Bartlett succeed in his suit; and if not, *why* ?

7. Is Mr. Bartlett living, and where ?

BRENTFORDIENSIS.

Brentford, 12 July 1821.

Monthly Mag. Sept. 1821, vol. lii. p. 109.

In the same number of the magazine we have, however, the following additional statement :—

*** *Another correspondent writes to the following effect :—*

Isaac Axford *never cohabited* with her. She was taken away from *the church door* the same day they were married, and he never heard of her afterwards.

Miss Chudleigh (the late Duchess of Kingston) was the agent employed to get Isaac to marry her, with a promise of a small sum of money. Isaac was then a shopman to Bolton the grocer on Ludgate Hill, and she lived with her father and mother at the corner of St. James' Market, and *the King frequently* saw her at the shop door as he drove by *in going to and from Parliament,* &c.

A Mr. Perryn of Knightsbridge was a relation of hers, and at his death left her forty pounds a year, *which Isaac had.*

Axford presented a petition to the King himself about her *in the Park on his knees,* as directed, but obtained but little redress.

The next account from *The Monthly Magazine* for October deserves special attention, not only because it gives a precise date and a precise locality for *her* marriage, but from its peculiarity of style, which smacks of the florid, if not elegant, style of Olivia Wilmot Serres :—

Further Particulars of Hannah Lightfoot, the Fair Quaker.

Hannah Lightfoot, when residing with her father and mother, was frequently seen by the King when he drove by going to and from the Parliament House. *She eloped in* 1754, and was married to Isaac Axford *at Keith's Chapel,* which my father discovered about three weeks after, and none of her family have seen her since, though her mother had a letter or two from her, but at last died of grief. There were many fabulous stories about her, but my aunt (the mother of H. Lightfoot) could never trace any to be true.

The above is a copy of a cousin of H. Lightfoot's letter to me on inquiry of particulars of this mysterious affair, and who is now living and more likely to know the particulars than any one else. The general belief of her friends was that she was *taken into keeping by Prince George* directly after her marriage to Axford, but never lived with him.

I have lately seen a half-pay cavalry officer from India, who knew a gentleman of the name of *Dalton* who married a daughter of this H. Lightfoot by the King, but who is dead, leaving several accomplished daughters, who, with the father, are coming to England; these daughters are secluded from society like nuns, but no pains spared in their education; probably on the arrival of this gentleman more light will be thrown upon the subject than now exists. The person who wrote the above letter is distantly related to me, and my mother (deceased some years) was related to H. Lightfoot and well knew her. I never heard her say any more than I have described already, except that she was short of stature and very pretty.　　　　　　　　　　　　　　AN INQUIRER.

Herts.

Monthly Mag. Oct. 1821, p. 197.

At the risk of trespassing somewhat heavily on the patience of the reader, I must before I close this branch of my subject call attention to a still fuller and more curious statement derived from the same source :—

Further details relative to the Fair Quaker.

The accounts published in your magazine relative to the Fair Quaker protected by the late King, differing in some respects from that which I have received from my relatives, who were her father's neighbours, I here give you their account.

St. James' Market, now pulled down, and absorbed in the improved state of the space between Pall Mall and Piccadilly at the end next the Haymarket, consisted before its dilapidation of two parts—a daily flesh market, and an open oblong space, on the east side of the other, called the country market for poultry and other country produce. Mr. Wheeler's house was the eastern corner house, and on the south side of this open part, and abutting upon Market Lane, a narrow lane which ran out of Pall Mall at the back of the Opera House, the lower end of which, as far as where Wheeler's house stood, is now covered over and made into an arcade. I well remember the shop, which after the decease of the old folks was kept by their son until the recent destruction. It was a linendraper's, and, as the principal part of the business lay with the country market people, the proprietors were accustomed to keep a cask of good ale, a glass of which was always offered to their customers.

At that time the ravages of the small-pox, unchecked by inoculation, left but few women who were not marked by its destructive powers; and the possessors of a fair unsullied face were followed by crowds of admirers. Such was the case of the Misses Gunning, who paraded the Mall in St. James' Park, guarded by a troop of admirers with drawn swords, to prevent the populace from encroaching on this hallowed spot sacred to gentility. The train of Miss W. as she passed to and from the meeting in Hemming's Row, St. Martin's Lane, was as numerous.

Being before the American War, the spirit of democracy had not introduced its levelling principles, and the royal family, the nobility, and even the gentry, were beheld with a kind of awe, which rendered the presence of troops or constables necessary for their protection. The royal family proceeded to the theatres in chairs, preceded only by a few footmen, and followed by about a dozen yeomen. When they went to the Opera they entered at the back door in Market Lane, which was near the country market; and therefore to avoid the length of that narrow passage, they passed up St. Alban's Street, skirted half the south of the market, and had then only a few paces to go down the lane. On these occasions the linens were taken out of the eastern window, and Miss W. sat in a chair to see the procession. The fame of her beauty attracted the notice of the Prince, and there were not wanting those who were ready to fan the flame and promote the connection.

One M—— and his wife then lived in Pall Mall; their house was the resort of the gay world, and the master and mistress were equally ready to assist the designs of the gamester or the libertine, and to conceal the gallantries of a fashionable female. To this man, familiarly known about the court by the name of Jack M——, the taking away of the Fair Quaker was committed.

Having received his orders, he proceeded to a watchmaker's shop on the east side of the country market, which commanded a good view of Wheeler's house, in order to reconnoitre. Repeating his visits, under pretence of repairing or regulating his watch, he discovered that a female named H—— frequently went to Wheeler's, and was well acquainted with the daughter; and the skilful intriguer was not long before he discovered that this woman was precisely fitted for his purpose.

Mrs. H—— had formerly been a servant at Wheeler's, since which she had been in service at one Betts', a glass-cutter in Cockspur Street, a large house facing Pall Mall, afterwards occupied by Collet, who married his widow, and before the recent destruction divided into two or three tenements—one a toolmaker's, another a watchmaker's. She had then been lately discharged from Betts'. Instead of going into another service, being a handsome woman, one of the apprentices named H—— married her, and she was almost immediately afterwards laid hold of by Jack M——, and readily engaged in procuring the Fair Quaker for the Prince, which her previous familiarity rendered easy. As the parents allowed their daughter to go out with Mrs. H——, interviews were thus obtained between the parties; and, on the elopement, it was found that

her clothes and trinkets had been clandestinely removed. Old Mrs.
Wheeler never recovered from the shock, and it was said she descended
the grave with a broken heart.

A handsome reward was no doubt given to Jack M——; and, on the
arrival of the Queen, a relative was, through his interest, appointed her
English teacher, and another has gradually proceeded since to the bench
of bishops. Mrs. H—— was said to have received 500*l.* for her share in
the business. Whatever might be the sum, her husband was by means
of it enabled to go into partnership with a fellow-apprentice, one S——,
who had then just returned from the East Indies, whither he had been
sent to one of the Nabobs along with some lustres to unpack and put them
up, and had thus accumulated a small sum. The one was a parish
apprentice, the other the son of a poor clergyman. They opened in oppo-
sition to their former master a shop at the corner of Cockspur Street and
Hedge Lane, afterwards called Whitcomb Street, which has also suffered
dilapidation, but the shop has reappeared in splendour.

Such is the history of this elopement, which I received from my
mother's relations, who had peculiar means of knowing the facts; as
also from a fellow-apprentice of H——'s, one Stock, who kept the
Lion and Lamb at Lewisham and whose wife (who afterwards married
a Mr. Peter White of that village) had also been a fellow-servant of
H——'s wife while at Betts'.

It was generally reported that the Fair Quaker was kept at Lambeth,
or some other village on the south of the Thames; a notion which probably arose from its being most customary with the Prince to ride out
over Westminster Bridge; but I have heard it said that she resided at
Knightsbridge, at a farm which supplied the royal family with asses'
milk. The house being retired from the road, and less than a mile from
the palaces, was well adapted for the purpose of private visits.

It is scarcely worth while to notice, that those who say the King saw
her as he passed to and from the Parliament House can have no knowledge of that part of London, and the situation of her father's shop.

Was not Mrs. H——'s maiden name Lightfoot? This might probably be ascertained by the register of St. Martin-in-the-Fields. As the
Wheelers would naturally use that name in relating the story, as being
that by which they could best designate her, has not some confusion
arisen between the two females concerned in the elopement?

T. G. H.

⁎ *We shall be glad of the anecdote of Osborne. We give ready inser-
tion to the above, but still rely on the communication from Warminster,
which described her as Wheeler's niece and the wife of Axford.—Monthly
Mag.* July 1822, vol. liii. pp. 517-8.

This letter from T. G. H. brought a further communication from W. H. of Warminster, who having,

as he says, begun the debate, claimed the privilege of the last word.

These are the last words which W. H. claims the privilege of having; and in which the Fair Quaker is no longer Wheeler or Lightfoot, but Hannah Whitefoot.

It is certain that the Fair Quaker's name was Hannah *Whitefoot*, and not Wheeler. I showed to Axford's own niece only yesterday the account given by T. G. H. She admits all he says about the situation of the shop, and the way Prince George got a sight of her in his frequent visits to the Opera House. To put a stop to these visits was the reason of her being married to Axford, who had paid her some attentions while he was shopman at a grocer's on Ludgate Hill. Mrs. S——, his niece, told me yesterday, that after they married they cohabited for a fortnight or three weeks, when she was one day called out from dinner, and put into a chaise and four and taken off, and he never saw her afterwards. Mrs. S—— says it was reported that the Prince had several children by her, one or two of whom became generals in the army.

When Axford, many years after, married a second wife, and it was reported that Hannah was still living, the late Lord Weymouth on enquiry asserted that she was not then living.

W. H.

Warminster, July 5.

Monthly Mag. Sept. 22, vol. liv. p. 116.

In *The Monthly Magazine* for Dec. 1822, vol. liv. p. 410, the discussion is carried on by a correspondent signed ' Curiosus, Clapham, Sept. 5,' who, after stating that he had dealt with Axford the grocer at the corner of the Old Bailey for nearly half a century—' a heavy and silent man,' who ' would never communicate a word on the subject '—says that the marriage with Axford was a matter of arrangement through the mediation of a certain eminent surgeon of that day, and doubts the cohabitation after the ceremony. That there were a few children—one who was in the army, but never

became a general officer, was said to have been seen
in company with Dr. M—— at Paris at the com-
mencement of the French Revolution, the Doctor
well knowing him and his history. 'Curiosus' then
refers to some other Quaker lady who had a strong
hold on the affections of the royal Adonis, but the
'attempt was instantly and peremptorily discounte-
nanced by the lady.'

Thus ends the history as far as *The Monthly
Magazine* is concerned.

Our next extract—a long one—is from a pamphlet
published in 1824, written by some one who had
obviously been behind the scenes during the exciting
period of the Queen's trial. It is written in a better
style than some other pieces of secret history which
we shall have occasion to notice :—

The Queen at this time laboured under a very curious, and to me unaccountable, species of delusion. She fancied herself in reality neither a
queen nor a wife. She believed his present Majesty to have been
actually married to Mrs. Fitzherbert; and she as fully believed that his
late Majesty George the Third was married to Miss Hannah Lightfoot,
the beautiful Quakeress, previous to his marriage with Queen Charlotte;
that a marriage was a second time solemnized at Kew (under the colour
of an evening's entertainment) after the death of Miss Lightfoot; and as
that lady did not die till after the births of the present King and his
Royal Highness the Duke of York, her Majesty really considered the
Duke of Clarence the true heir to the throne. Her Majesty thought
also that the knowledge of this circumstance by the ministers was the
true cause of George the Fourth's retaining the Tory administration
when he came into power.

How the Queen came seriously to entertain such romantic suppositions
as these, it is not for me to know. It may be perhaps regarded as a
melancholy proof of the principles and abilities of some persons surround-
ing royal personages; but that she did entertain them I know well, and
let any of her Majesty's friends contradict me if they can. If they do,
and they require me to mention my author, I will do so if called upon
in a proper manner and in a proper place.

Indeed I was myself requested to call upon Mrs. Hancock to make enquiries relative to what she might think on the subject, as she had the pleasure of being intimate with Miss Lightfoot. I was also requested to see the person who styles herself (whether justly or unjustly signifies little to the subject) Princess of Cumberland, to know *if any of her real or presumed documents contained reference to that subject.*

Having no knowledge of Mrs. Hancock, who, I understand, is a highly respectable lady, I could not presume to take so great a liberty as to call upon her upon a subject so extraordinary. But knowing a friend who was intimately acquainted with the latter, I requested him to ask a question which I felt I could have no right to ask myself. The answer was, *that ' all her documents were in her own possession.'* This reply I sent to the personage I have so often alluded to, and I also transmitted the following intelligence, with which Sir William —— was so obliging as to favour me; viz. that Miss Hannah Lightfoot, when young, lived with her father and mother, who, at the time of Prince George's residence at Leicester House, kept a linendraper's shop at the corner of St. James's Market.

When the Prince went to St. James's, the coach always passed that way, and seeing the young lady at the window occasionally, he became enamoured of her, and employed Miss Chudleigh, afterwards Duchess of Kingston, to concert an interview. From this time frequent meetings were secured at the house of a Mr. Perrhyn of Knightsbridge, who was, I believe, Miss Lightfoot's uncle.

The Court is said to have taken alarm at these circumstances; and Miss Chudleigh, seeing the danger likely to ensue, privately offered to become a medium of getting the young lady married. With this view she got acquainted with a person who was a friend of the Lightfoot family, named Axford, and who lived at that time on Ludgate Hill. This person consented to pay his addresses to Miss Lightfoot, and even nominally to marry her upon the assurance of receiving with her a considerable dower.

Miss Lightfoot is supposed to have given in to the plan, for she was married at *Keith's Chapel in* 1754, though the marriage was never consummated; for Miss Chudleigh, who had contrived the match (probably with the sanction of all parties), took her into a coach as she came out of the church door, and the husband pocketed the dower, but never saw his wife afterwards. The mother indeed heard from the daughter once or twice before she died, and Axford made enquiries after her at Weymouth, Windsor, and Kew; and once is even said to have presented a petition to the King on his knees as his Majesty was riding one day in St. James' Park, but no certain account of her was ever known from the period of her marriage day.

She was taken, it is supposed, under the protection of Prince George *under an assumed name,* and is said to have had a daughter subsequently married to a gentleman of the name of Dalton or Dalston, who afterwards received an appointment from the East India Company in Bengal, whither he went, and where he died, leaving three daughters.

Mr. Axford, in the meantime, not hearing anything of his wife, and probably considering his marriage not strictly binding, since it had never been consummated, married another lady, named Bartlett, then living at Keevil, in North Wiltshire; and, after the expiration of fifty-eight years, died without ever being able to obtain any intelligence of his first bride.

Three things are very remarkable in the history of this lady—viz. that she was never personally known to the public; that her residence while alive was never publicly known; and that so strict a secrecy was observed at her death, that it is nowhere upon known record, though it has been said that she died of grief in the parish of St. James, and was buried under a feigned name in the parish of Islington, where probably she may rest without a stone to tell the history either of her life, death, guilt, innocence, splendour, or misfortune. — *An Historical Fragment relative to Her late Majesty Queen Caroline*, pp. 44-50.

There are one or two points in this statement which deserve notice. First, it is clear that as early as 1824 Mrs. Wilmot Serres was mixed up with the story; and next, what could Mrs. Handcock, who was only a friend of this mysterious Hannah Lightfoot, mean by 'her documents were in her own possession?' What documents could she possibly have? Has not the writer rather confounded Mrs. Wilmot and Mrs. Handcock's replies, and was it not the former who spoke of ' her documents?'

Eight years after this—namely, in 1832—the scandal was revived in that notorious collection of libels, *The Authentic Records of the Court of England for the last Seventy Years*, where, after telling how the Prince of Wales, when passing through St. James' Street and its immediate vicinity, ' saw a most engaging and prepossessing young lady dressed in the garb usually worn by the female Quakers,' it is stated that he became so enamoured of her that—

At length the passion of the Prince arrived at such a point that he felt assured his happiness or misery depended upon his receiving this lady in marriage. Up to this period the Prince had at all times exhibited and expressed his high regard for all virtuous undertakings and engagements; but he well knew that virtue could seldom be found in a court. . . . . .

One individual only was the friend of the prince on this occasion, and in the year 1759 the prince was *legally* married to this lady, Hannah Lightfoot, at Curzon Street Chapel, May Fair. The only *positive* witness of royal faith was the prince's *eldest* brother Edward, Duke of York, &c. &c., who at all times was the adviser or friend of George, and whose honour the Prince knew was inviolable.—Pp. 2 and 3.

But terrible events followed, says the *Authentic Recorder*—

The ministry soon became aware that some alliance had been formed, and *their irritation was soon followed by exclamation!*

Nay, not only did they cry, ' Oh, fie, you naughty boy ! ' which is, I suppose, what the writer means by ' followed by exclamation,' but they made him marry another wife, and

Miss Lightfoot was disposed of during a temporary absence of his brother Edward, and from that time not any *satisfactory* tidings have reached those most interested in her welfare. One thing only transpired, which was, that *a young gentleman* named Axford was offered a large amount, to be paid upon the consummation of his marriage with Miss Lightfoot, which offer he accepted. . . . The king was greatly distressed to ascertain the fate of his much-loved and *legally*-married wife, the Quakeress; and he entrusted *Lord Chatham to go in disguise* and endeavour to trace her abode; but the search was fruitless, and again the King was almost distracted.—Pp. 5–7.

But according to this *Authentic Recorder*, not only was the King distracted, but the Queen, who knew his secret, was no less so; and, in 1765, insisted upon being again married, and ' Dr. Wilmot !! by his Majesty's appointment, performed the ceremony at their palace at Kew. The King's brother Edward was present upon this occasion, as he had been *on the two former ones !* '

The book we have here quoted contains many other

passages equally clear and consistent, but it detracts
perhaps from its value as an authority, that the
publisher of it was indicted for a libel of a revolting
character upon the Duke of Cumberland, contained
in a ' deposition ' which a certain individual ' was in-
clined to give.'   The very individual on whose pretended deposition the libel was founded was, however,
produced in court and utterly denounced it, and the
publisher was consequently convicted.   The book is
then *said to have been suppressed.*

But the story we have just told from the *Authentic Records* is *repeated* in another work of similar
character, which also bears the date of 1832; though,
as it will presently be seen, there is reason to believe
it was not *circulated,* for it can scarcely be said to
have been published, till a year or two after.   This is
*The Secret History of the Court of England, &c.   By
the Right Honorable Lady Anne Hamilton, Sister of
his Grace the present Duke of Hamilton and Brandon,
and of the Countess of Dunmore.*

Mr. Jesse speaks of these *two* literary productions
as being composed by persons *not ill-informed in the
secret history of the court*—a point on which we by no
means agree with Mr. Jesse; and we are surprised
that, as he seems to have especially consulted them,
it never struck him that, as Puff says in *The Critic,*
' when these' writers, not ill-informed in the secret
history of the court ' *do* agree their unanimity is
wonderful,' and that having the books before him he
should not have discovered that *The Secret History*
(with which the lady whose name appears on the

title-page had no more to do than Hannah Lightfoot herself) is only *The Authentic Records* newly revised.

This the *Quarterly Review*, in reviewing the latter, showed as long since as April 1838 (vol. lxi. p. 406): where the Reviewer, after expressing his belief that the publication of the *Authentic Records* and *Secret History* was not 'instigated so much by individual malice as by a reckless and shameless desire of *gain* acting upon low, brutal, and malignant natures,' tells us how the books were *circulated*, not published :—

> The former publication, which is about the size usually sold for seven or eight shillings, was circulated, *under the cloak*, at the modest price of 1*l.* 1*s.*, and the extravagance of the sum was a decoy to make the credulous suppose that there must be something very *piquant* in so dear a volume. The present work is—on the same principle—retailed by a woman, who in the dusk comes to the door and offers *Lady Anne Hamilton's Journal* at the same modest price of *one* guinea per volume.*

We presume the game was not very profitable; for some years afterwards the remainder of the book was offered by, probably, the very same woman to a well-known bookseller, who declined the purchase, and copies were to be procured a few years since at a very trifling price.

But, says Mr. Jesse, 'singularly enough, we find more than one of the statements contained in *The Authentic Records* and in *The Secret History* endorsed by the respectable authority of a no less well-informed person than William Beckford;' adding,

* The identity of the books was very clearly shown in *Notes and Queries* of the 9th March 1867, by a gentleman who has kindly permitted me to print it in the Appendix. (See Appendix A.)

'His account, it is true, differs in detail from some others.' And this opens up two curious questions— first, what degree of reliance can be placed upon the 'Conversations' in question? secondly, where did Beckford pick up the information with which, in the present case, he *mystified* the reporter of them?

A correspondent of *Notes and Queries*, ' Calcuttensis,' asked lately upon what authority do the *Conversations* rest? The answer is simple—upon that of Mr. Cyrus Redding, a gentleman upon whose good faith every reliance may be placed. But, in spite of that, I do not believe they are to be depended upon as evidences of Mr. Beckford's real opinions. Having heard this often stated, I have applied to a gentleman who knew Mr. Beckford extremely well, for information upon the subject. After saying that he agreed with me in my estimate of the value of the *Conversations*, and stating that for the last ten years of Mr. Beckford's life not a day between the months of January and July passed without his being two or three hours in his company, he adds :—

I have no recollection of his having mentioned Hannah Lightfoot, but I do remember distinctly talking with him frequently about Junius, and believe that he attributed the authorship to Francis. As to Dr. Wilmot, he used to make facetious observations about him in connexion with Olivia Wilmot Serres. But Mr. Beckford *delighted in mystification*, and would often tell me hilariously how he had humbugged people.

And then proceeds to express his belief that Beckford often exercised this perverse humour on the reporter. Now, what did Mr. Beckford profess to believe? His story, as reported in the *New Monthly Magazine*,

vol. lxxii. p. 216 (see *Notes and Queries*, 1st S.
x. 228), was that the parties were '*married by Dr.
Wilmot, the author of Junius!* at Kew Chapel, in
1759, William Pitt (afterwards Earl of Chatham)
and Ann Taylor being the witnesses, and for aught I
know the document *is still in existence*!'

It certainly is. It is one of several produced at
the late memorable trial, and pronounced by the
Lord Chief Baron 'gross and rank forgeries,' and
which are, we believe, impounded in Sir James
Wilde's Court at the present moment.

Is there any sane man in England who believes
that Wilmot was Junius; or that a man of Mr. Beckford's sagacity and intelligence gave credence to such
an absurdity? This statement alone is sufficient to
show that the *Conversations*, however faithfully they
may have been reported, are of no value as historical
evidence.

The allusion to the certificate proves clearly that
Mrs. Olivia Wilmot Serres was the authority which
suggested to Beckford this *figment*: though in which
of her many pamphlets she first introduced Dr.
Wilmot as the party who performed the marriage
ceremony between the Prince and Hannah Lightfoot
I have not yet been able to ascertain.

Dr. Wilmot's name was, as far as I have traced,
first introduced into connection with the subject
before us in the *Authentic Record* and *Secret
History*; and this will probably suggest to my
readers, as it has done to myself, the probability that
Mrs. Serres was mixed up with these disreputable

books.   True, that Dr. Wilmot is in these books merely stated to have re-married the royal pair, and is not represented as having anything to do with the marriage of the fair Quaker.   The latter was more likely an after-thought, suggested, as the lady would probably have said, by the *discovery of the certificates*!

I do not know when these documents were first given to the world ; but in 1858 they were printed in *The Appeal for Royalty*, and reprinted in the same work last year, and as literary curiosities, and giving completeness to the materials for a full history of the scandal, are here printed in full :—

April 17th, 1759.

The marriage of these parties was this day duly solemnised at Kew Chapel, according to the rites and ceremonies of the Church of England, by myself,

J. WILMOT.

GEORGE P.
HANNAH.

Witnesses to this marriage—
W. Pitt.
Anne Taylor.

———

May 27th, 1759.

This is to certify that the marriage of these parties, George Prince of Wales to Hannah Lightfoot, was duly solemnised this day according to the rites and ceremonies of the Church of England, at their residence at Peckham, by myself,

J. WILMOT.

GEORGE GUELPH.
HANNAH LIGHTFOOT.

Witnesses to the marriage
of these parties—
William Pitt.
Anne Taylor.

———

George R——.   Whereas it is our Royal command that the birth of Olive, the Duke of Cumberland's daughter, is never made known to the nation during our reign ; but from a sense of religious duty, we will that she be acknowledged by the Royal Family after our death, should she

survive ourselves, in return for confidential service rendered ourselves by
Dr. Wilmot in the year 1759.

Kew Palace,
May 2nd, 1773.
(Signed)   CHATHAM.
WARWICK.

Indorsed, London,
   June 1815.
Delivered to Mrs. Olive Serres
   by Warwick.
      Witness, EDWARD.*

Hampstead, July 7th, 1768.

Provided I depart this life, I recommend my two sons and my daughter
to the kind protection of their Royal Father, my husband, his Majesty
George III., bequeathing whatever property I may die possessed of to such
dear offspring of my ill-fated marriage. In case of the death of each of
my children, I give and bequeath to Olive Wilmot, the daughter of my
best friend, Dr. Wilmot, whatever property I am entitled to or possessed
of at the time of my death.—Amen.

(Signed)   'HANNAH' REGINA.

Witnesses—
   J. Dunning.
   William Pitt.

I will not occupy space and weary the reader
by here recapitulating what various correspondents
in *Notes and Queries* have related about Hannah
Lightfoot,† but will endeavour to tell the story
according to the evidence which has been produced
by the various authorities for it.

Once upon a time there was a fair Quaker, whose
name was Hannah Lightfoot. No, Anna Eleanor
Lightfoot. No, Whitefoot. No, Wheeler.

Well, never mind what her name was; her father
was a shoemaker, who lived near Execution Dock,

---

* This is the signature of the late Duke of Kent.
† They will be found in 1st S. viii. 87, 281; ix. 233; x. 228, 328,
430, 532; xi. 454; 2nd S. i. 121, 322; x. 80; xi. 117, 156; 3rd S. iii.
88, &c.

Wapping. No, he was a linendraper, and lived at St. James's Market. No, that was her uncle.

But these are mere trifles. She no doubt had a name, and lived somewhere.

Well, the Prince saw her as he went from Leicester House to St. James's. No, that's wrong; it was as he went to the Opera. No, you are both wrong; it was as he went to the Parliament House!

Never mind where he saw her: he did see her, and fell in love with her; and, as neither his mother the Princess Dowager nor Lord Bute looked after him, and he was then nearly sixteen years old, he married her in 1754! No, that's not right; it was in 1759.

But it does not matter when he married; he did marry her at Keith's Chapel in May Fair. No, it was at Peckham. No, it was at Kew.

No, that is all a mistake. Her royal lover never married her. Isaac Axford married her and left her at the chapel door, and never saw her after that. Yes, he did; they lived together for three or four weeks, and then she was carried away *secretly* 'in a carriage and four,' and he never saw her after that.

Wrong again. It was the King from whom she was so strangely spirited away, and he was distracted; and *sent Lord Chatham in disguise* to hunt for her, yet he could never find her.

No, that's all wrong. It was Axford who could not find her, who petitioned the King to give him back his wife at St. James's. No, that was at Weymouth. No, it was *on his knees in St. James's Park, as directed.*

But would it not be a sheer waste of time to continue this list of contradictions? No two blacks will ever make a white. However large a mass of contradictions may be, the formula which shall convert it into one small historical truth has yet to be discovered. Until that time arrives, I shall rest convinced, and trust the readers of these hasty notes will share my conviction, that the story of Hannah Lightfoot is a fiction, and nothing but a fiction, from beginning to end.

Fortunately for the cause of truth, the law of evidence which regulates Sir James Wilde's court does not govern the court of historical enquiry. In this latter, principals may be examined; and being enabled, therefore, without the assistance of Mr. Hume, to call George III. as a witness, I venture to think that his Majesty will prove distinctly the utter groundlessness of the Lightfoot scandal. Of course, the evidence is not direct, for in all probability the King had never heard of Hannah Lightfoot. But it is scarcely less important, showing as it does his opinion on such matters, and the improbability of his having been engaged in anything of the kind.

In the valuable collection of *Letters of George III. to Lord North*, lately published by Mr. Murray, we find the King writing to his friend and minister with reference to the Duke of Cumberland's intrigue with Lady Grosvenor (Letter 45, Nov. 5, 1770):—

I cannot enough express how much I feel at being in the least concerned in an affair that my way of thinking has ever taught me to behold as highly improper.

This is language perfectly consistent, not only with what Waldegrave and Walpole have told us, but with all we know of George III.; but utterly inconsistent with the truth of the Lightfoot story.

Again, in a letter to Lord North (No. 654, Dec. 10, 1780), consulting him, as he expressly says, 'as a friend, not a minister,' about the establishment which was then to be formed for the Prince of Wales, the King says:—

I thank Heaven, my morals and course of life have but little resembled those too prevalent in the present age; and certainly of all the objects of this life, the one I have most at heart is to form my children that they may be useful examples and worthy of imitation.

This is not the language of a man who had been engaged in a disreputable intrigue with the fair Quaker.

But a still more remarkable declaration on the part of the King (with reference to this question) is contained in his letter to Lord North on the subject of the Prince of Wales's connection with Mrs. Robinson. The letter is so striking that I give it without abridgement:—

(No. 689.)

Windsor, Aug. 28, 1781,
40 min. pt. 9 A.M.

I am sorry to be obliged to open a subject to Lord North that has long given me much pain, but I can rather do it on paper than in conversation; it is a subject of which I know he is not ignorant. My eldest son got last year into a very improper connection with an actress, and a woman of indifferent character, through the *friendly* assistance of Lord Maldon; a multitude of letters passed, which she has threatened to publish unless he, in short, bought them of her. He had made her very foolish promises (*sic*) which, undoubtedly, by her conduct to him, she entirely cancelled. I have thought it right to authorise the getting of them from her, and have employed Lieut.-Col. Hotham, on whose discression (*sic*) I could depend, to manage this business. He has now brought it to a conclusion, and has her consent to get the letters on her receiving 5,000*l.*—undoubtedly an enormous sum; but I wish to get my son out of this shameful scrape. I desire you will therefore see Lieut.-Col. Hotham, and settle this with him. I AM HAPPY AT BEING ABLE TO SAY THAT I NEVER WAS PERSONALLY ENGAGED IN SUCH A TRANS-ACTION, WHICH PERHAPS MAKES ME FEEL THIS THE STRONGER!

Is it to be believed that had there been one atom of foundation for the Lightfoot scandal Lord North would have been ignorant of it; or that the King would have given utterance to the important decla-ration—'I am happy at being able to say that I never was personally engaged in such a transaction?'

Having been most positively assured that Mr. Burn had, in the course of those researches to which we are indebted for his valuable publications on the subject of 'Parish Registers,' actually found a cer-tificate of the marriage of the Prince and Hannah Lightfoot, I ventured to write to Mr. Burn on the subject. He informs me that he never saw any such certificate; that he does not believe that any such marriage took place; that if it was at Keith's Chapel, it must have been before March 25, 1754, when marriages ceased there; and reminds me that after that date any such marriage would be void.

QUEEN CHARLOTTE AND THE CHEVALIER D'EON.

Having, as I trust, successfully vindicated George III. from the slander which connected his name with that of Hannah Lightfoot, I venture to attempt a similar act of justice to his exemplary wife.

Scandal against Queen Elizabeth is as old as the hills, but scandal against Queen Charlotte, except in the libellous pages of *The Authentic Record* or *The Secret History* was, to me at least, a thing unheard of until some months since, when my attention was called to a libellous calumny in which her Majesty's name was mixed up with that of no less notorious a person than the Chevalier D'Eon. This disgusting stuff was to be found in the *Mémoire* of that celebrated diplomatist, by M. Gaillardet, published in two octavo volumes as long since as 1836.

All the endeavours I then made to obtain a copy of that book, for the purpose of seeing on what authority M. Gaillardet made such an extraordinary charge, having failed, I was compelled, like Mr. Micawber, to ' wait till something turned up.'

That something has turned up very unexpectedly in the shape of a new edition of M. Gaillardet's *Mémoire,* which its preface has rendered one of the most extraordinary books which I have ever met with.

In this preface, which is headed 'Un Acte de Contrition et un Acte d'Accusation,' M. Gaillardet tells us that in 1835 he obtained from some members of the Chevalier's family many papers and documents calculated to throw new light upon his history; and at the same time from the Duc de Broglie, then Minister of Foreign Affairs, and M. Mignet, Directeur des Chancelleries, permission to ransack the Archives for the whole period of the Chevalier's political career. One would have thought any biographer might have been satisfied with such an accumulation of new materials.

It was not so, however, with M. Gaillardet. But he shall tell how he set to work in his own words:—

Mais j'eus alors un tort qu'expliquent ma jeunesse et le genre de littérature dans lequel je m'étais essayé. J'avais vingt-cinq ans, et je venais de faire jouer le drame de la Tour Nesle, avec Alexandre Dumas; je ne rêvais que péripéties compliquées, amours tragiques, et sécrets ténébreux. La vie du Chevalier d'Eon, telle que je venais de la parcourir, si accidentée qu'elle fut, me parut encore trop simple pour n'avoir pas une partie cachée, qui échappait à toutes les récherches, et qui devait être d'autant plus graves qu'on en avait anéanti les traces avec plus de soin. Je me disais qu'un homme,—car c'était bien un homme,—qui avait rempli des missions secrètes sous le costume de femme, avant de prendre officiellement ce costume, avait dû nécessairement avoir des aventures, ou piquantes, ou terribles, ayant un rapport forcé avec le dénoument de sa carrière. Je crus, même de bonne foi, avoir *trouvé la piste de la plus grave de ces aventures amoureses dans les lettres d'audiences nocturnes accordées par la jeune reine d'Angleterre au Chevalicre d'Eon, aprés la paix de* 1763, paix aussi nécessaire que honteuse pour la France, au sujet de laquelle la presse anglaise accusa le ministere et la cour de s'être laissés corrompre ou séduire, par la diplomatie française.

Mon imagination travailla donc, et il résulta de ce travail que mon livre se *composá d'une partie authentique et d'une partie romanesque.* Malgré cela, ou peut-être à cause de cela, il se vendit beaucoup; à tel point que, depuis longtemps, on n'en trouve plus un exemplaire en librairie.

The italics are mine. M. Gaillardet tells us he was often requested to reproduce a new edition— 'reduite à la partie purement historique et sérieuse,' but for various reasons felt disinclined to the task. Some years afterwards he saw the announcement of a volume on the subject of the Chevalier D'Eon by M. Louis Jourdan, rédacteur du *Siècle*, but the title, *Un Hermaphrodite*,* led him to pay no attention to it till he met M. Jourdan one day at the office of the *Siècle*, when he asked him to send it to him. This M. Jourdan promised to do—a promise which, however, was never fulfilled. Some time afterwards accident brought *Un Hermaphrodite* under the notice of M. Gaillardet, who found the author in his preface boasting of the numerous masses 'de documents à peine soupçonnés,' which he had had to wade through in the preparation of his book, while he passed over without notice M. Gaillardet's previous labours in the same direction. But let M. Gaillardet now tell his own story:—

Or, quelles ne furent ma surprise et ma stupéfaction, lorsque je retrouvai le production la plus complète de mes Mémoires, non seulement dans la fond, mais aussi dans la forme, non seulement dans leur partie authentique, mais encore et surtout dans leur partie fictive. En effet, c'est surtout ce que j'ai inventé, ce qui est faux historiquement parlant qui à séduit l'auteur de *l'Hermaphrodite* et lui a paru *constituer la réalité la moins contestable.*

---

* M. Gaillardet knew that the Chevalier was a man, but the mistake in his first edition was his supposing him to be 'le type de Faublas.' In his second edition, which is a very interesting book, and we presume one which may be depended upon, he explains the strange conduct of the Chevalier in certain matters to have arisen from his love of notoriety, and the fact that 'il était à peu près, sinon tout à fait *vierge.*'

Here the italics are M. Gaillardet's.

Of the 301 pages which constitute *Un Hermaphrodite*, 222 are taken word for word from the *Mémoire* of M. Gaillardet (whose name is never once mentioned), the few remaining pages being an abridgment of his historical introductions.

We will not follow M. Gaillardet through his curious list of pure fictions, the creation of his own imagination, which prove the grossness of the plagiarism, but we will give his account of one of these in his own words and with *his own moral*:—

La même bénignité d'esprit à fait adopter à mon plagiarie, comme articles de foi, TOUT CE J'AVAIS CRU ET DIT DES AMOURS DU CHEVALIER D'EON AVEC SOPHIE-CHARLOTTE, DUCHESSE DE MECKLEMBOURG DEVENUE REINE D'ANGLETERRE. Il reproduit toujours textuellement pages 81 et 83 les réflexions que je mets dans la bouche de mon héros sur ce sujet. UNE REINE À DEVORRER ÉTAIT, À CE QU'IL PARAIT, UN MORCEAU TROP APPÉTISSANT POUR QU'IL Y REGARDÂT DE PRES.

I have called the reader's special attention by small capitals to the more striking parts of this unblushing announcement. When I say that in *Un Hermaphrodite*, which M. Gaillardet assures us is taken almost word for word from his book, this atrocious fiction of the intrigue between Queen Charlotte and D'Eon is referred to over and over again; that we have in it minute accounts of their stolen interviews; that George IV. is again and again spoken of as the son of the Chevalier, and not of George III.; that the King's jealousy is dwelt upon; that we have minute details of his discovering D'Eon and the Queen together at two o'clock in the morning at an assignation; that all the love passages and the recriminations are fully detailed as part of the fictions which M. Gaillardet describes himself as having 'cru et dit'—with what overwhelming force do his own words apply to himself, ' UNE REINE À DEVORER ÉTAIT À CE QU'IL PARAÎT UN MORCEAU TROP APPÉTISSANT POUR QU'IL Y REGARDÂT DE PRÈS.'

Here then we have this atrocious scandal disavowed by its originator, who, in the new edition of his book, which has for its running title *Le Verité sur la Chevaliere d'Eon*, of course omits all allusion to it.

But it may be said, the story is so absurd, the book in which it is propagated so little known, that it is surely never worth taking notice of it. My answer is, that a calumny such as this should always be denounced and exposed; and more especially as it has been put into print, and that, too, in a book which professes to be founded on historical materials. In the latter case the wrong is indefinitely increased; for it is liable to be quoted without suspicion, and received as true without question. This very scandal has been referred to as recently as 1858, not in any obscure publication little likely to be referred to, but in no less popular, well-known, and frequently consulted book than the *Nouvelle Biographie Générale*, tome xvi. p. 103, n. 1. It is true that the editor of the *Biographie* doubts the truth of the story; but nevertheless in this work of recognised authority M. Gaillardet's figment is treated, not as the gross libel which it is, but as the deliberate statement of one who had made the life of the alleged partner of the Queen's misconduct his special study.

I trust I may be permitted, by way of postscript, to give a curious picture of bookmaking in Paris as detailed in the preface and epilogue of the book before us. When M. Gaillardet discovered the daring piracy of which he had been the victim, he commenced proceedings to recover damages against M. Dentu, the publisher, and M. Louis Jourdan, the author of *Un Hermaphrodite*. M. Jourdan pleads as an excuse, But I did not write the book. It was written by a young friend of mine, then unknown, 'aujourd'hui honorablement placé dans le journalisme,' who, being in want of money, at my suggestion that he should examine into and write the Life of the Chevalier d'Eon, undertook the task, and after some time brought me a large MS. which I read, revised, and signed. The journalist E. D., who really *appropriated* M. Gaillardet's fictions, pleads as his excuse his youth and his belief that they were historical facts, and, as such, common property. Sterne would, we think, scarcely have applied to the bookmaking world of Paris his well-worn saying—' They manage these things better in France.'

DR. WILMOT'S POLISH PRINCESS.

There is one chapter in the Wilmot-Serres romance which, though slightly touched upon by the Attorney-General in the late *cause célèbre*, deserves a few remarks; one personage who every now and then comes on the scene, 'like a shadow and so departs,' of whose presence, however, for reasons which will appear hereafter, it is desirable some record should be preserved. I allude to the Princess Poniatowski, whom Dr. Wilmot is alleged to have married, and by whom he is said to have become the father of the supposed Duchess of Cumberland.

This Princess is like Dame Quickly—one 'don't know where to have her.' We first get a glimpse of her in 1813, in Mrs. Serres' *Life of Dr. James Wilmot* (an impudent and foolish attempt to prove him the writer of *The Letters of Junius*), where, in a note at p. 116, we read—

When the Princess of Poland visited England, Dr. Wilmot attended her to the university. She valued our author exceedingly during her residence in England, and *invited him to the Court of Poland*; she frequently corresponded with him after her departure from this kingdom.

In 1815 Lord Warwick communicated to Mrs. Serres the startling and agreeable fact that she was the daughter of the Duchess of Cumberland—and not only to Mrs. Serres, but also to the Duke of Kent, who seems to have been no sooner let into this grave secret than he was seized with the same mania for writing certificates and declarations for which all the parties to it are so remarkable;* a mania which manifested itself in making its victims forget their grammar and orthography, spell ' offspring ' *orfspring*; and all alike endeavour to hide the mysteries with which they were familiar under the most transparent veil. Thus we find Dr. Wilmot cautiously concealing the names of Junius, Lord Shelburne, and Wilkes, under the occult symbols of Ju——s, L——d S——ne, J. W——; while Lord Chatham, in a document in which he pledges himself not to betray the Duke of Cumberland's second marriage, writes about ' the laws against b——y,' and the Duke of Kent in like manner writes, ' F——t M——ge ' and ' R——l birthright,' for fear anybody should guess he meant ' first marriage ' and ' royal birthright.' ·

But though, in 1815, Lord Warwick announced to Mrs. Serres that she was the daughter of the Duchess of Cumberland, he seems very unaccountably to have omitted the additional interesting fact that she was the granddaughter of a Princess. Strange omission this of Lord Warwick; but still the fact must have been forgotten, for two years after Mrs. Serres had ascertained her descent from the Duchess of Cumber-

---

* Dr. Smith, the counsel of Mrs. Ryves, is reported in *The Times* of June 2 to have stated that about seventy documents would be produced, containing forty-three signatures of Dr. Wilmot, sixteen of Lord Chatham, twelve of Dunning, twelve of George III., thirty-two of Lord Warwick, and eighteen of the Duke of Kent. What an ingenious mode of keeping State secrets !

land, we find her, in a pamphlet published in 1817, entitled *Junius, Sir Philip Francis Denied*, asserting, at p. 6—' Dr. Wilmot was NEVER MARRIED,' and drawing from that circumstance additional arguments in favour of his identity with Junius.

As far as we have been able to ascertain, Mrs. Serres did not put forth any claim to be a descendant from a Polish Princess until 1821, when she made the following announcement in *The British Luminary*, which was understood to be the Princess of Cumberland's official organ; at which time also she declared her right to the throne of Poland:—

Dr. Wilmot, in early life, was a Fellow of Trinity College; he was a high-spirited, independent character, of great talent, and the friend and favourite of many of the young nobility then at Oxford. Stanislaus, afterwards King of Poland, was at that time studying at Oxford, and Dr. Wilmot became intimate with him. Stanislaus had a SISTER living with him (Princess Poniatouski), a very beautiful young creature; and from the intimacy which subsisted between the prince and the doctor, he was frequently in company with the young princess; a mutual attachment took place between them; but the princess was not rich; and they were at length privately married. Only a few confidential friends were acquainted with the transaction, for had it been generally known, the doctor would have lost his fellowship and his other high pretensions.

In due time the princess presented Dr. Wilmot with a daughter. Some family and political matters separated the parties for a while. He doated upon his lovely child, who, we believe, was placed under the care of Mrs. Payne, the sister of the doctor and the wife of Captain Payne.

All the time the doctor could spare from his studies and different occupations he devoted to his beloved and interesting child, who grew up the beautiful image of her royal mother, with a mind as superior as her person, and at the age of eighteen the Duke of Cumberland and the Earl of Warwick became her admirers; at length the earl gave way to the duke, and on March 4, 1767, they were married by Dr. Wilmot at the house of his friend, Lord Archer, in the presence of Lord Brook (afterwards Lord Warwick) and Mr. Addez, which was only known to a few persons about the Court.

The apparently happy duke and his lovely bride lived in hopes that they should soon be allowed to make their marriage public; but in the year 1771 a transaction took place which proved a cruel deathblow to the young duchess, for she never recovered the effect. . . . ! ! !

Young, amiable, and beautiful, and tenderly attached to the duke, she took leave of him and went to Warwick in a state of misery not to be described. A premature birth at seven months was the consequence. On Tuesday, April 3, 1772, she gave birth to the Princess Olive at the house of Mrs. Wilmot, in Jury Street, in the town of Warwick. The Earl of Warwick and Dr. Wilmot were both present, which fact is confirmed by their separate affidavits.

The unfortunate duchess was conveyed to France in a state scarcely to be described, where she afterwards died in a convent of a broken heart.—*Gent.'s Mag.*, July 1822, vol. xcii. Part ii. pp. 35-6 (quoted from *The British Luminary* of Dec. 16th, 1821).

But the mystery is at length cleared up. We are now told that Lord Warwick did not reveal the whole story of her birth and connection in 1815, but delivered to her a sealed packet, which was not to be opened until after the death of the King; but which, with strange disregard to so solemn an injunction, was opened in 1819, though the King did not die till 1820; and that packet for the most part related to the marriage of Dr. Wilmot with the Princess Poniatowski.

However, as Mrs. Serres' grandmother, the Princess Poniatowski, gave birth to a daughter on June 17, 1750, we are very glad to find for the lady's sake that she was married. We presume this event took place in 1749; but, unfortunately, Dr. Wilmot, fond as he seems to have been of writing down all the great secrets with which he was entrusted, seems never to have taken sufficient care of the Polish interest of his descendants, and has not certified *where*, *when*, or *whom* he married.

In the *Appeal for Royalty*, it is said (p. 7) Dr.
Wilmot ' contracted a private but legal marriage with
the Princess of Poland, DAUGHTER of Stanislaus, last
King of that country.' As the author of the *Appeal*
had access to all the documents, how comes it that,
while Mrs. Serres in 1821 declared the lady to have
been a SISTER of Stanislaus, the *Appeal*, published in
1858 and republished in 1866, declares her to have
been his DAUGHTER? Dr. Smith, Mrs. Ryves's counsel,
who ought to know, having doubtless studied the case
very closely, returns to the original version, and says
the lady was the Princess Poniatowski, SISTER of the
King of Poland.

On the 2nd June, Dr. Smith produced to the Court
an article in the *Biographie Universelle*, for the purpose of proving the biography of Dominic Serres.
Had the learned Doctor, in turning over the leaves of
that useful book, glanced his eye at the Life of Stanislaus, and been startled by the announcement—

' Ce prince n'avait pas été marié ? '

There the statement is, at any rate; and the fact is
so. Stanislaus never was married. But this is not
all. The favourite of Catherine was, no doubt, a remarkable man ; but he would have been a very
remarkable man indeed if, born in 1732, he was the
father of a marriageable daughter in 1749.

So much for Dr. Wilmot's marriage with a DAUGH-
TER of Stanislaus.

Let us now see whether the story which Dr. Smith
adopted—namely, that this supposititious Princess was

the SISTER and not the DAUGHTER of Poniatowski—is a bit more consistent than the one which he rejected.

If the reader will refer to Niesiecki's *Herbarz Polski* (article 'Poniatowski,' vol. vii. pp. 376–378, edit. 1839–46), the best authority, we believe, on the subject, he will find that Count Poniatowski, afterwards King of Poland, had four brothers and only two sisters. Of these, the eldest, Louisa, born in 1728, married one of the Zamoyski family, and left a daughter married to a Count Mniszech. The younger, Isabella, born in 1730, married Clement Branicki, and died without issue.

So much for the assertion that Dr. Wilmot married a SISTER of the King of Poland.

We have thus shown that the whole story of this pretended marriage is clearly a pure invention, by proving that in 1813, Mrs. Serres knew nothing of it ; that in 1815, according to the *Appeal*, she was informed of 'all the particulars of her birth and connections;' that in spite of this, in 1817, she declared that 'Dr. Wilmot was never married;' that in 1821, she announced his marriage to a SISTER of Poniatowski; that in 1858 and 1866, this sister was in the *Appeal* transformed into a DAUGHTER; who in the Ryves case was again transformed into a SISTER; that Poniatowski was never married, and consequently had no DAUGHTER; that neither of his sisters could have been married to Dr. Wilmot. It would therefore be waste of time and space to touch upon the absurdity of converting this mythic daughter or sister of *Count* Poniatowski—who was not *elected* King of Poland till

1764—into a *Princess* of Poland in 1749 ; or to show
where Poniatowski was when the pretended marriage
took place; or to prove that his visit to England did
not occur till five years after the date which Mrs.
Serres assigned to it.

Parodying what the Lord Chief Justice said of the
certificates of the pretended Lightfoot marriage, that
they were ' gross and rank forgeries,' it may safely be
declared of the two versions of the Wilmot-Poniatow-
ski marriage—they are ' gross and rank fabrications;'
and Mrs. Serres' statement in 1817, that ' Dr. Wilmot
was never married,' remains one of the few statements
made by her entitled to credit.

Whilst hurriedly penning these lines, our attention
was attracted to the date mentioned above as that of
the birth of the Princess Olive—' Tuesday, April 3,
1772.' It is very seldom, in connection with this
case, that one gets anything quite so precise and defi-
nite. The importance of a royal birth of course justi-
fies and accounts for the minute and unwonted par-
ticularity. Happening to have at hand Mr. Bond's
excellent Perpetual Calendar, we thought we would
test this Tuesday, the third of April. No sooner said
than done. For 1772, Mr. Bond's contrivance at
once informed us that D was the Dominical Letter,
and that the 1st April was on a Wednesday; the 3rd
was therefore a Friday, and not a Tuesday. Could
it be Tuesday, the 13th? No, the 13th was on a
Monday. Or Tuesday the 23rd? No, the 23rd was

on a Friday. How was it to be accounted for? We soon discovered. The person who endeavoured to ascertain the day of the week, not having Mr. Bond's little chronological machine at hand, and not being a very profound chronologer, calculated the date accord ing to the old style, under which the 3rd of April 1772 would have been a Tuesday, but, unfortunately for him or her, the style was changed in 1752, twenty years before the date assigned to this illustrious birth.

LORD CHATHAM AND THE PRINCESS OLIVE.

I have lately been reminded of an interesting conversation I once had with the late Mr. J. Wilson Croker, in which he maintained and illustrated one of his favourite canons, that there are no tests of truth so severe and so much to be depended upon as dates; and I propose, as a supplement to what has just been read, to apply this test to a few of the documents produced in support of the remarkable claim of Olive Wilmot to the title of Princess of Cumberland. I select for the purpose of being submitted to such test those Papers which Lord Chatham is represented to have witnessed or countersigned, so far as the collections of *Chatham*, *Grenville*, and other correspondence, published since Mrs. Serres put forth her absurd claims, furnish the means of testing the dates of these *Documents* by genuine Papers.

Lord Chatham's signature as William Pitt is affixed to the certificates of the pretended marriage of the Prince of Wales with Hannah Lightfoot, first celebrated, as it is alleged, at Kew, on 17th April 1759, and afterwards, on the 27th May, at Peckham. Now, the 27th May was Sunday,—a day, one would think, rather unlikely (though I speak in great ignorance of the domestic arrangements of Royal households) for a young Prince to select for absenting himself from his family for the purpose of getting married. Sunday, 27th May 1759, was, moreover, a day one would believe especially inconvenient for the Great Commoner to be engaged in such a transaction; as we find in the *Grenville Correspondence*, Vol. i. p. 301, a letter from him to Mr. Grenville, dated 'Hayes, Monday, May 28, .1759,' announcing 'Lady Hester's safe delivery that morning of a son.'* I do not much depend upon this, but taken in connection with what follows, it deserves, I think, the reader's attention.

The celebrated statesman, Mr. Pitt, having twice witnessed the Lightfoot marriage, was obviously the fittest person in the world to witness that of the Duke of Cumberland and Olive Wilmot, which took place, according to the certificate, on the 4th March 1767, in the presence of 'George R.; Chatham; and Warwick.' Lord Chatham must have made great exertions to have affixed his signature to this interesting document, for on the preceding day—3rd March 1767—as we learn from *Chatham Correspondence*, Vol. iii. p. 228, that having occasion to write to the King (I presume not expecting to have the pleasure of meeting him on the following evening at Lord Archer's, where the marriage was solemnised), he employs Lady Chatham to write for him and tell his sovereign that, 'He is most unhappy to continue out of a condition to attend his Majesty's most gracious presence;' while on the 7th, the King writes to him (obviously keeping very secret their pleasant meeting on the 4th), 'I can-

---

* 'William Pitt . . . . was born,' remarks Lord Stanhope, 'on the 28th May 1759, at Hayes, near Bromley, in Kent.'—*Life of Pitt*, i. 1.

not conclude without desiring to learn 'how you continue, and insisting on .your not coming out till you can do it with safety' (*Chatham Correspondence*, iii. 229).

Though the marriage took place at Lord Archer's, by some unaccountable oversight that nobleman omitted to sign the certificate, or, to use the word of the *Appeal for Royalty* :—

Still there was wanting the signature of one witness of the marriage; and in order, therefore, to put the fact beyond the reach of cavil, a third certificate * was drawn up and signed in the following terms :—

'Lords Chatham and Archer solemnly protest that the marriage of Henry Frederick Duke of Cumberland and Olive my daughter, the said Duke's present Duchess, was solemnised legally, at the latter nobleman's residence, Grosvenor Square, London, by myself, March 4th, 1767.

(Signed) 'J. WILMOT.

(Signed) 'CHATHAM.
     'ARCHER.
'3 Nov. 1767.'

Unfortunately, the place where this document was dated is not stated. We will supply the omission. In a letter from Mr. Augustus Hervey to Mr. Grenville, dated at 'Bath,' that very day, 'Nov. 3, 1767,' we read, 'Here Lord Chatham is, and goes out every day on horseback when the weather lets him.' So that Lord Archer and Dr. Wilmot jogged together down to Bath to get Lord Chatham's signature to a third certificate of Olive Wilmot's marriage ! Well may the author of the *Appeal to Royalty* exclaim :—

That man must be a more than usually intrepid infidel who, in the face of such documents as these, will venture to disbelieve that the Duke of Cumberland was lawfully married to Miss Wilmot on the 4th March 1767.

---

* The first certificate was signed 'J. Wilmot' only.

I am afraid a good many readers must by this time be included in the class of ' more than usually intrepid infidels.'

Mr. Pitt having witnessed Queen Hannah's marriage, it was natural that she should select him as a witness of her will. It was executed at Hampstead, July 7th, 1768, and was witnessed by Dunning and Pitt. The great Commoner must have shown extreme devotion to this one of his royal mistresses, and must have put himself to *serious* inconvenience to sign 'this touching paper,' as it is styled by the writer of the *Appeal* (iii. 32), for it appears from the *Chatham Correspondence*, that on the 16th June he was at Hayes, ' so much indisposed as to be quite unable to write ; ' and on the 16th July (Ibid. 331), Lady Chatham writes to Lord Radnor on account of ' Lord Chatham continuing much indisposed and unable to write.' How severely Queen Hannah must have reproached herself when she saw the sick and suffering Earl enter her presence in obedience to her mandate!

The next documents printed in the *Appeal*, which are signed by Chatham, are dated on the 1st May and 2nd May 1773 respectively. The first is a declaration by which Lord Chatham binds himself to pay £500 yearly to the Duke of Cumberland's infant daughter. This paper bears the signatures of the King, J. Wilmot, Robert Wilmot, and Lord Chatham, and is dated, as I have said, ' this first day of May 1773,' but where executed does not appear. The document of the following day, dated ' Kew Palace, May 2nd, 1773,' is the State paper by which the King commanded that, '*in return for confidential services rendered our-selves by Doctor Wilmot in the year* 1759,' Olive's birth should be kept secret during his reign, but be acknowledged by the Royal family after his death. This paper is countersigned by Lord Chatham and Lord Warwick.

As it appears, by the recently-published *Letters of George the Third to Lord North*, that the King was at this time residing, *not at Kew*, but at the Queen's house, one wonders that the document should have been dated at *Kew*; but we will not stop to enquire into that, or why the next document, of the 21st of the same month, which created Olive Duchess of Lan-caster, and which also is witnessed by Lord Chatham, should be dated from St. James's. Our present ques-tion is with Lord Chatham, who, writing from Burton Pynsent to Lord Shelburne, on the 24th May 1773 (*Chatham Correspondence*, iv. 264), makes mention of 'our most welcome guest, Lord Stanhope, who left us on Friday last.' Now, the 24th May in 1773 was a Monday; the ' Friday last ' was consequently the very 21st May on which day Lord Chatham was at Burton Pynsent, and could not have countersigned the Royal warrant at St. James's. It is also evident, from the preceding letters, that he had been there for a consi-derable time, and could not have countersigned the documents of the 1st and 2nd of May.

Are my readers surprised if I confess that my infi-delity becomes more and more ' intrepid,' and that I feel assured that, after what I have shown them, they will attach just as much value to these certificates as I do,—and no more ?

APPENDIX A.

THE 'AUTHENTIC RECORDS' AND 'SECRET HISTORY.' *

Every historical reader must feel grateful to Mr. Thoms for his able commentary upon the myth of Prince George's marriage with 'Hannah Regina.' It adds strong confirmation to my own belief that the entire fiction was wrought out, with some ingenuity and with great pertinacity, by Olivia Wilmot Serres; her groundwork having probably been, as your correspondent Mr. Hyde Clarke suggests at p. 156 of this volume, some exploded vulgar rumour or street ballad which appears to have been popular at the end of last century, when Mrs. Serres was thirty years old, and was probably an active penwoman, her first acknowledged biographical work, *The Life of the Author of the Letters of Junius*, having been published in 1813.† I think that a copy of *What! what! d'ye call him, Sir, and the Button-maker's Daughter*, would interest many readers of ' N. & Q.' One of two conclusions must, I think, be clear in the minds of all who have

---

* Reprinted by permission of the author from *Notes and Queries*, 3 S. xi. 196.
† She published *Flights of Fancy* in 1805.

investigated the subject—either (1) that Mrs. Serres
wrote the accounts of Hannah Lightfoot, which appeared most opportunely in the *Monthly Magazine* in
1821 and 1822; her acknowledged petition to the
Crown, with a view to establish her legitimacy as
daughter of Henry Frederick, Duke of Cumberland,
having been presented in 1819; and her *Statement
to the English Nation, including certificates and con-
firmations of the Princess Olive's royal parents'
marriage, and her birth*, having been published in
1822. Further, that she was the author of *An
Historical Fragment relative to her late Majesty Queen
Caroline*, which appeared in 1824; and that the two
works (or rather the two editions of the same work),
the *Authentic Records of the Court of England*, and
the *Secret History of the Court of England*, came from
the same active and unscrupulous pen; or that (2)
Mrs. Serres was in direct communication with the
writers of all these works, who reproduced her statements in her own words.

Let us compare the following quotations:—

The Life of the Author of the Letters of Junius, the Rev. James
Wilmot, D.D., late Fellow of Trinity College, Oxford; Rector of Barton-
on-the-Heath and Aulcester, Warwickshire, and one of his Majesty's
justices of the peace for the county . . . . By his Niece, Olivia Wilmot
Serres.

Dr. Wilmot lived in habits of friendship and confidence with some of
the most distinguished characters of the age. Among them were Mr.
Grenville, Lords Northington, Shelburne, and Sackville, together with
the celebrated Mr. Wilkes, Mr. Thurlow, and Mr. Dunning. The late
Bishop of Worcester, Lords Plymouth, Archer, Sondes, Bathurst, Grosvenor, Craven, and Abington were on terms of intimacy with him, more
particularly the three first-named noblemen. He was well acquainted
with many members of the Administration from 1766 to 1773; and there
is no question but his political information was derived from these sources.

Then take the expressions used in the *Secret History of the Court of England*, published nineteen years later (page 48):—

Numerous disquisitions have been written to prove the identity of Junius; but, in spite of many arguments to the contrary, we recognise him in the person of the Rev. James Wilmot, D.D., Rector of Bartou-on-the-Heath, and Aulcester, Warwickshire, and one of his Majesty's justices of the peace for that county.

Dr. Wilmot was born in 1720, and during his stay at the university became intimately acquainted with Dr. Johnson, Lord Archer, and Lord Plymouth, as well as Lord North, who was then entered at Trinity College. From these gentlemen the doctor imbibed his political opinions, and was introduced to the first society in the kingdom.

We have, then, a facsimile of what most readers will accept as a genuine Serres document:—

'I have this day completed my last letter of Ju—s, and sent the same to L—d S—ne. J. W—. March 17, 1772.'

I regard it as almost a matter of certainty that these two sets of passages were written by the same person; and who but Mrs. Serres would describe Dr. Wilmot in the terms made use of in the second quotation?

I have just finished a very careful perusal of the *Secret History of the Court of England*, published in 1832. The Lightfoot scandal forms an integral part of the whole scheme of the work, which is evidently written from beginning to end by the same hand. It may be well to mention that the correctness of Mr. Jesse's impression, that the *Authentic Records* and the *Secret History* were written by different persons, is positively disproved by more than one statement in the latter work. We are told at page 156 that—

In a former work of ours, called the *Authentic Records of the Court of*

England, we gave an account of the extraordinary and mysterious murder of one Sellis, a servant of the Duke of Cumberland, which occurred this year. In that account we did what we conceived to be our duty as historians—we spoke the TRUTH! The truth, however, it appears, is not always to be spoken, for his Royal Highness instantly commenced a *persecution* against us for a ' malicious libel.'

Again, at page 196:—

In this character only did we publish what we believed, and *still believe,* to be the *truth,* in our former work of the *Authentic Records,* and which we have considerably enlarged upon in our present undertaking.

The *Historical Fragment* quoted by Mr. Thoms at p. 110, and the *Secret History,* are, I believe, our only ' authorities ' for the statement that Queen Caroline was acquainted with the ' fact ' of George the Third's marriage with the fair Quaker.

The statements stand as follows in the two works. In the *Historical Fragment* we are told—

The Queen [Caroline] at this time laboured under a very curious, and to me unaccountable, species of delusion. She fancied herself in reality neither a queen nor a wife. She believed his present Majesty to have been actually married to Mrs. Fitzherbert; and she as fully believed that his late Majesty George the Third was married to Miss Hannah Lightfoot, the beautiful Quakeress, previous to his marriage with Queen Charlotte; that a marriage was, a second time, solemnised at Kew (under the colour of an evening entertainment) after the death of Miss Lightfoot; and as that lady did not die till after the births of the present King and his Royal Highness the Duke of York, her Majesty really considered the Duke of Clarence the true heir to the throne.

All this may be gathered, piecemeal, from the *Secret History.*

In a letter, stated by this slanderer, at page 228, to have been addressed by Queen Caroline to her husband, we have the words—

To you it is well known that the good King, your father, has invariably treated me with the most profound respect and proper attention;

and his Majesty would have done me more essential service long since, had it not been for the oath he gave to Lord Chatham, to preserve from all *public* investigation the connexion formed in 1759 with the Quakeress.

At p. 83 :—

In the early part of this year [1786], the Prince *was married* to Mrs. Fitzherbert.

The Queen insisted on being told if the news of his marriage were correct. 'Yes, madam,' replied he ; 'and not any force under heaven shall separate us. If his Majesty had been *as firm* in acknowledging *his marriage*, he might *now* have enjoyed life, instead of being a misanthrope as he is.'

At page 107 we have, in a copy of a letter alleged to have been written to the Princess Caroline of Brunswick, by George Prince of Wales, 1794, the following words :—

Learn, then, the *secret* and *unhappy* situation of the prince whom they wish you to espouse. I cannot love you ; I cannot make you happy ; my heart has long ceased to be free. She who possesses it is the only woman to whom I could unite myself agreeably to my inclinations, &c.

It is pretended that George the Third wrote at the same time to the Princess Caroline, and to her mother the Duchess of Brunswick. In the former forgery he is made to say—

I have explained to my sister the probable difficulties which my son George may mention ; but they must not have any weight in your mind and conclusions.

In the latter—

He may please to plead that he is already married ; and I fear he will resort to any measure rather than an honourable marriage.

At page 37 we read—

Early in the year 1765 the Queen was pressingly anxious that her marriage with the King should again be solemnised; and, as the Queen was then pregnant, his Majesty readily acquiesced in her wishes. Dr. Wilmot, by his Majesty's appointment, performed the ceremony at their palace at Kew. The King's brother, Edward, was present upon this occasion also, as he had been on the two former ones.

I believe that, henceforward, the name of Hannah Lightfoot will cease to have any place in the secret history of England; but I trust that the editor of ' Notes and Queries ' will not allow the enquiry to be closed until every statement regarding this mythical personage shall have been thoroughly sifted. I have again gone over the statements which appeared in the First and Second Series of ' Notes and Queries.' The only assertions which still appear to need canvassing are those made by. E. D. (1st S. x.ᵥ 430), and by Mr. G. Steinman Steinman (2nd S. i. 322). These are confirmatory of the statement made in the letter signed ' An Inquirer,' *Monthly Magazine*, Oct. 1821, cited by Mr. Thoms at pages 90, 91 of your current volume, to the effect that Dr. James Dalton, of the Madras Medical Service, married a daughter of Hannah Lightfoot by the King, and had by her a daughter, Caroline Augusta, who was, in 1854, the wife of Daniel Prytherch, Esq., of Abergoh, Caermarthen, who has had by her no less than fourteen children. After the manner of all these evidences, ' Inquirer ' of 1821 and E. D. of 1854 are quite irreconcileable on the subject of Dr. Dalton's family. The former tells us that he had ' several accomplished daughters, who, with the father, are coming to England; these daughters are secluded from society like nuns, but no pains spared in their education.' It is distinctly stated that the mother was then dead.

The other authority states that Dr. Dalton left ' by this lady four children—Henry Augustus, of the Royals, or 1st Foot Regiment; Hawkins Augustus, of the Royal Navy; Charlotte Augusta (all three of whom died a few years afterwards); and Caroline Augusta.' It rather singularly occurred that, a few weeks since, I sent a paper relating to Hannah Lightfoot to the late venerable John D'Alton of Dublin. Writing to me on the 10th of January last, only ten days previous to his decease, he used the following striking expressions:—

I may say briefly, for indeed I have not strength to meander far over a sheet of paper, that concerning the Princess Olive of Cumberland has been for years by-gone, put forth to the public on vouchers and *stilts* that have broken down in the sand, and I would say it was well such a superstructure failed. I confess that I have little regard for romantic schemes that seek to set aside the succession of such sovereigns as the late William the Fourth, and our own best Queen that ever wielded the sceptre of England.

I had then forgotten the name of Dr. Dalton; but I think that, had the above story not also been a myth, the great genealogist *of his own name* would not thus have noticed a pamphlet entitled, *The Princess Olive of Cumberland, Hannah Lightfoot, and the Author of the Letters of Junius.*

CALCUTTENSIS.

LONDON
PRINTED BY SPOTTISWOODE AND CO.
NEW-STREET SQUARE

EVERY SATURDAY, 24 PAGES,

Price FOURPENCE, of all Booksellers, or stamped to go by Post, FIVEPENCE,

NOTES AND QUERIES;

CONTAINING EVERY WEEK A VARIETY OF AMUSING ARTICLES
ON THE FOLLOWING SUBJECTS:—

ENGLISH, IRISH, AND SCOTTISH HISTORY,
illustrated by original Communications and inedited Documents.

BIOGRAPHY, including Unpublished Correspondence
of Eminent Men, and Unrecorded Facts connected with them.

BIBLIOGRAPHY, more especially of English Authors,
with Notices of rare and unknown Editions of their Works, and Notes on
Authorship of Anonymous Books.

POPULAR ANTIQUITIES AND FOLK LORE, pre-
serving the fast-fading relics of the Old Mythologies.

BALLADS AND OLD POETRY, with Historical and
Philological Illustrations.

POPULAR AND PROVERBIAL SAYINGS, their
Origin, Meaning, and Application.

PHILOLOGY, including Local Dialects, Archaisms,
and Notes on our old Poets.

GENEALOGY AND HERALDRY, including Histories
of Old Families, completion of Pedigrees, &c.

MISCELLANEOUS NOTES, QUERIES, AND RE-
PLIES on points of ECCLESIASTICAL HISTORY, TOPOGRAPHY, FINE ARTS,
NATURAL HISTORY, MISCELLANEOUS ANTIQUITIES, NUMISMATICS, PHOTO-
GRAPHY, &c.

RECENT OPINIONS OF THE PRESS.

'In my puzzle, I applied to that most useful periodical, *Notes and Queries*, and obtained an immediate answer.'—DEAN OF CANTERBURY in *Good Words*, Feb. 1866.

'That useful resuscitant of dead knowledge—yclept *Notes and Queries*—the antiquaries' newspaper.'—*Quarterly Review*, No. 184, p. 329.

'The invaluable running commentary with which *Notes and Queries* accompany every current topic of literary interest.'—*Saturday Review*, April 14, 1866.

NOTES AND QUERIES is published every Saturday, price 4d.; or stamped to go by Post, 5d. It is also issued in Monthly Parts; and in Half-Yearly Volumes, each with copious Index, price 10s. 6d. cloth boards.

The Subscription for Stamped Copies for Six Months, forwarded direct from the Publisher (including the Half-Yearly Index), is 11s. 4d., which may be paid by Post-Office Order, payable at the Strand Post-Office, to WILLIAM GREIG SMITH.

A Specimen sent for Five Stamps.

---

32 WELLINGTON STREET, STRAND, W.C.,
And by order of all Booksellers and Newsmen.

www.ingramcontent.com/pod-product-compliance
Lightning Source LLC
Chambersburg PA
CBHW031929060726
47496CB00008BA/2775